THE
WILD WEST
SHOW

THE WILD WEST SHOW

Phil Carradice

Pont

First published in 2013 by Pont Books, an imprint of
Gomer Press, Llandysul, Ceredigion, SA44 4JL

ISBN 978 184851 666 3

A CIP record for this title is available from the British Library.

© Copyright text: Phil Carradice, 2013

Phil Carradice has asserted his moral right under the
Copyright, Designs and Patents Act, 1988
to be identified as author of this work.

This book is published with the financial support of the
Welsh Books Council.

Printed and bound in Wales at
Gomer Press, Llandysul, Ceredigion, SA44 4JL

Contents

Chapter One

A PARADE PASSES BY

'They're coming! They're coming!'

Sam was the first to hear it, long before the other people crowding and jostling beside him. To begin with, it was little more than a distant whisper but soon a great current of excitement was rolling up the street and rippling from pavement to pavement.

'They're coming!' The words broke in a great roar against the grey walls of Cardiff Castle, like the waves Sam saw surging up the Channel each day and smashing against the walls of the dock.

People were standing four or five deep along the street but Sam pushed and struggled until he reached the front of the crowd.

'Can you see them?'

Sam glanced up at the speaker. He recognised him as Mr Tomkins, the owner of a sweet and toy shop at the bottom of St Mary Street. His temper, Sam knew, was short and he had often chased Sam and the other street boys away from his shop window.

For a moment Sam thought the man was speaking to him but then he realised that Mr Tomkins's words had been meant for the wife waiting obediently beside him, not the dirty little urchin who stood expectantly at his feet. Sam knew that nobody ever gave him a second glance – not unless he was putting filthy fingerprints onto the plate glass of a sweet-shop window.

Suddenly there was a new noise amongst the shouting and calling. 'Listen!' said Mr Tomkins.

Sam turned his head towards the sound. A distant drumbeat – tom-toms or war drums, he guessed – was being carried towards him on the morning air.

And now, at last, they came. First there were mounted cowboys – the rough-riders – powerful-looking men on strong black horses. Volleys of bright sparks flashed into the air each time their horses' hooves struck the cobblestones.

Then there were the flatbed wagons on which the Indians rode, all beating on their drums or, from time to time, leaping down into the roadway to race up to spectators and make them shy away in panic. They were followed by dozens of covered wagons, the prairie schooners that had carried the pioneers and settlers across the American West.

And all the time, men and women, each of them dressed in bold checked shirts and buckskin jackets and leggings, paraded up and down the lines of astonished and fascinated watchers. They shook hands with everyone, laughing and handing out leaflets. One of them thrust a slip of paper into Sam's hands.

'Here, son,' he drawled. 'This tells you everything you want to know.'

Sam stared at the paper, turning it over and over in his hands.

'What does it say?' asked Mrs Tomkins.

Sam shook his head. He had never learned to read.

'Give it here,' snarled Mr Tomkins, impatiently snatching the leaflet from his fingers.

'Read it out, Mr Tomkins,' said somebody from the crowd behind them. 'Go on. Tell us what it says.'

Self importantly, Tomkins pulled a pair of wire-framed spectacles from his waistcoat pocket and gave them a quick polish on the end of his tie before perching them on the bridge of his nose. Carefully, he read the information. 'It says,' he announced at last, 'that there will be a show, a Wild West show, tomorrow at three o' clock in Sophia Gardens. Indians, cavalry, rough-riders, shooting demonstrations, it'll all be there.'

He screwed up the paper into a tiny ball and tossed it carelessly into the gutter.

'That's going to be worth seeing,' said a voice from the crowd. 'I'm definitely going.'

The parade was still in full flow. A brightly coloured stagecoach, pulled by six panting horses, clattered past.

'The Deadwood Stage,' said Mr Tomkins, pointing at the coach. 'They say Buffalo Bill himself drove it in front of old Queen Victoria when they came for her Golden Jubilee, fourteen or fifteen years ago.'

Gaily dressed women, their faces painted and rouged, were leaning out of the stagecoach windows. They laughed and called out to the spectators.

Mrs Tomkins sniffed disdainfully and turned her head away. 'Saloon girls,' she announced. 'How disgusting!'

The stagecoach was followed by a troop of US cavalry, their blue uniforms contrasting sharply with the red-and-white headdresses of the Indians who rode alongside them.

'Someone told me,' commented Mrs Tomkins, 'that the Indians who massacred General Custer at the battle of the Little Bighorn are in the show. Perhaps Sitting Bull will be here too.'

Sam glanced up. He'd heard of Sitting Bull. He was the chief and medicine man who had masterminded the Indian victory over Custer, the American general. Could he really be part of this amazing show?

Mr Tomkins shook his head scornfully at his wife. 'Not unless he's got stronger magic than anyone ever thought possible. He died fourteen years ago, killed by Indian police. Imagine that, done in by his own people.'

More than a little pleased at having been able to display his knowledge, Tomkins turned away. Sam was disappointed. Maybe not Sitting Bull, then, but there was still so much to see. He turned back to watch the parade.

More wagons – Mexican this time – trundled past.

Then, as if from nowhere, came six giant cows, herded along by their keepers. Sam stared at the great hairy beasts. He'd never seen animals like these before.

'Buffalo,' announced Mr Tomkins. 'There are thousands of them in the American West, just roaming wild. That's how Buffalo Bill got his name, buffalo hunting. He used to go out onto the prairie and shoot them for food.'

The idea of killing such magnificent beasts was horrible, Sam thought. But then, he supposed, people had to eat and in a wilderness like the Wild West there would be no shops or restaurants to give folks what they wanted. And anyway, who was he to worry about where food came from? He'd gone hungry far too often to bother himself with things like that.

He had no time to ponder because, out of nowhere, a man mounted on a snow-white horse was galloping up the street towards him.

'It's Buffalo Bill,' called someone. 'Buffalo Bill Cody.'

Buffalo Bill was dressed, like all the other cowboys, in a buckskin jacket. But this one was almost white in colour and it was covered with bright shining stars and red ribbons. Every few yards, he would pull up, sweep off his wide-brimmed Stetson hat and wave it at the crowd. 'Come and see the show,' he called, smoothing down the white goatee beard on his chin. 'Tomorrow at three, ladies and gentlemen. There's room for everyone – as long as you can pay your entrance fee.'

The crowd erupted in laughter and began to cheer.

Buffalo Bill was wonderful, Sam thought, a real live rough-rider, like no one he'd ever seen before. He remembered all he'd ever heard about him from the other street boys, how Bill used to ride, delivering mail for the Pony Express, covering hundreds of miles in a single day – perhaps on the very same horse he was riding now. They said that he had killed 4,000 buffalo to provide meat for the men building the new railways across America. He'd been a scout for the US army and been a personal friend of George Armstrong Custer and General Phil Sheridan.

Sam knew he had to see the next day's show. But how? He had no money, no friends to help him out. His parents had died so long ago he could barely remember them. He just knew that Buffalo Bill's Wild West show was the greatest thing ever to happen in Cardiff. And somehow or other he was going to see it.

Just then, the crowd on either side of him fell silent. When Sam looked up Buffalo Bill was sitting astride his horse, barely two feet away. And he was staring directly at Sam.

Bill leaned forward in the saddle. His blue eyes, sharp and piercing, twinkled as he winked at the boy. A strand of his long brown hair fell across his cheek like a pencil mark. 'Here, son. This is for you.'

He held out his hand and Sam edged warily forward. Buffalo Bill pushed a slip of cardboard into his palm.

'What is it?' asked Sam.

Bill smiled. 'It's a ticket, a free ticket, for tomorrow's show. I guess you can do with it.'

He dug in his spurs and the white horse reared up onto its hind legs. Then he was gone, charging away up the street and waving to the hundreds of spectators who still waited at the roadside.

Sam had eyes only for the ticket. He held it in his hand, gazing at the lurid drawing on its face – Buffalo Bill fighting at least two dozen war-painted Indian warriors. A free ticket? He could hardly believe it.

After a few moments, he felt, rather than saw, the envious gaze of Mr and Mrs Tomkins and others in the crowd. 'It's not fair,' he heard Mrs Tomkins complain. 'Why should he get a free ticket? The rest of us have to pay. So should he. Get it off him, John.'

From the corner of his eye Sam saw Mr Tomkins push himself forward and reach out for the ticket. His arm snaked through a gap in the crowd. 'Here, boy,' he said. 'That's no use to you. You wouldn't appreciate it even if they did let you in.' His fingers began to curl around the precious piece of card but Sam was in no mood to be browbeaten or bullied. He shrugged himself away, protecting the ticket with his thin body.

'Go away,' he shouted. 'Get off!'

'Give that to me, damn you!' cursed Mr Tomkins and pushed forward again.

Sam lashed out with his foot. His boots were old and full of holes but they were heavy and his kick caught Mr Tomkins full on the shin. The man howled in pain and fell to the ground.

Sam didn't wait a moment longer. He took to his heels, racing away through the crowd. Even when he was a hundred yards away, he could still hear Mr Tomkins shouting in pain and fury.

Chapter Two

THE WILD WEST SHOW

That night, Sam kept his treasured ticket close to his chest – literally. He pushed it inside his ragged shirt and felt it warm against his skin. And all night long, as he lay under a piece of sacking in an empty doorway, he kept one hand on the precious piece of card.

He was awake early, foraging amongst the rubbish outside the market hall, trying to find something to eat. He had almost resigned himself to another hungry day, when his eyes fell on three copper coins lying together in the gutter.

They must have been dropped by a careless porter or an early market shopper, he thought. Sam didn't care where they came from. He dived for the coins and scooped them up into his pocket. 'It must be my lucky day,' he whispered to himself as he skipped past the market stalls. 'First money to buy breakfast and then the Wild West show this afternoon.'

He bought a tin mug of coffee and two soft white rolls from a stall in the Hayes. The trader looked at him sharply, as if trying to work out where he had stolen the money for such luxuries but when Sam held out the coins he did not refuse them and swept them quickly out of the boy's palm.

*

Sam was at Sophia Gardens long before the three o'clock deadline. Buffalo Bill's showmen had put up tepees, tall pointed wigwams that reached high into the air. They were arranged around the edges of the park and in front of these strange-looking contraptions sat groups of Indian men, women and children.

The sharp, sweet smell of burning wood came from their campfires. For some reason the smell of those fires made Sam feel lonely and sad. He hardly ever thought about family and home, things he couldn't really remember, but now, suddenly, he wanted nothing more than to sit before those blazing flames with people he loved and cared about and who cared about him. 'Don't be stupid,' he told himself. 'That's never going to happen.'

He wandered through the camp, gazing in wonder at the strange sights. The tepees were made of cowhide and were decorated with drawings of deer, horses and buffalo. Circular and triangular shapes were painted onto their sides, decorations that he didn't understand but which dazzled his eyes with their brightness.

Bows and arrows, war lances and rifles lay propped up on the grass outside each tent. He stopped outside one and tried to peer in through the open flap.

'Do you want to look inside?'

Sam turned. A small Indian girl, black hair braided into bunches on either side of her head, was standing staring at him.

'Sorry?'

'I said, would you like to see inside my tepee?'

Sam nodded and followed her into the darkness. When his eyes became used to the light he was able to see that everything in the tent was incredibly neat and tidy. Bedrolls were stacked against the walls and the ground was carpeted by bright red-and-yellow rugs. Little pockets stitched to the tent walls held an array of knives, spoons, bone needles and other implements.

'This is amazing,' said Sam. 'Do you live in here?'

The girl laughed. Her eyes sparkled. 'Of course not. This is just for the show. Buffalo Bill – Mr Cody – expects us to sit here while the visitors come to stare – like you just did. I sleep with my mother in one of the covered wagons. That's where we all live.'

Sam stared at the girl. 'Are you a real Indian?' he asked.

'What's an Indian?' she said. 'That's just a name the white men, the settlers and the army, gave us when they started to push us off our lands. I'm a Cherokee. That's an Indian tribe. There's lots of tribes like ours, all over the Great Plains. Sioux, Arapahoe, Apache, lots and lots of them.' She stared intently at Sam, as if trying to work out if he was really interested. Satisfied, she carried on talking. It was clearly a speech she'd given many times before or one she'd heard the grown-ups making. 'We all live our own lives, each tribe. We're different, all of us. We've got our own traditions and history. The tribe is what's important. We hunt as a tribe, fight as a tribe, live as a tribe – not as "Indians".'

Sam looked puzzled.

The girl put out her hand and took his arm. 'It's a bit like you living in Wales. Over here you've got different tribes, too – Welsh, English, Irish, Scottish. That's what Bill says, anyway. You're all different, aren't you? Sometimes you come together, just like we did at the battle of Little Bighorn. That's how we beat General Custer – though we called him Yellow Hair. That's what made Sitting Bull such a great leader. He pulled us all together to fight against Custer.'

She smiled at Sam. 'If you want to call us anything, call us Native Americans. After all, we lived in America long before the white men came.'

They went back out into the sunlight. People were beginning to arrive in greater numbers now, walking through the Indian camp towards the arena where the Wild West show would take place. There was a sense of expectation in the air.

'My name's Running Water,' said the girl. 'What's yours?'

Sam grinned at her. 'Running Water? What sort of a name is that?'

The girl shrugged. 'It's a Cherokee name. My mother says our tribe was camped alongside a river when I was born; I was called after the stream. So what's your name, then?'

'Sam, Sam Thomas.'

'Sam Thomas,' laughed the girl. 'What sort of a name is that?'

Sam laughed with her and he realised that he liked this tiny girl with her ruddy brown face and twinkling grey eyes. But he knew that time was going fast and he had an appointment that nobody was going to make him break. 'I've got to go,' he said. 'Maybe I'll see you again.'

'Are you going to the show?'

Sam nodded. 'Buffalo Bill gave me a ticket.'

Running Water turned back towards her tepee. 'He often does things like that. Look out for me in the show. I'm usually in the first of the wagons.'

For the next few hours Sam sat, enchanted, as members of the Wild West show appeared in front of him. It was as if they were performing just for him. The other spectators – and there must have been close on 20,000 of them, Sam thought – might as well have been somewhere else.

In the big parade, Sam spotted Running Water sitting in the back of the leading wagon. He thought about waving to her but knew she'd never see him in the crowd.

He watched, entranced, as Custer's Last Stand was acted out by bands of cavalry soldiers and Indians. Volley after volley of rifle fire echoed around the park. The air was filled with flying arrows and soon banks of acrid gun-smoke lay like early-morning mist across the battlefield.

Next a band of Indians attacked a log cabin and tried to seize the Deadwood Stage whilst Buffalo Bill charged around the arena on his white horse.

Best of all was the sharp shooting of Annie Oakley. The famous markswoman shot glass balls out of the air, never missing the mark. She even fired backwards over her shoulder, using a mirror to sight the target. Sam had never seen anything more skilful.

'The first time the Wild West show came to Britain,' he heard someone say, 'she shot a cigar out of the mouth of the Kaiser.'

'Shame,' came the retort. 'She'd have done better to miss the cigar and hit him.'

Sam had heard the older street boys talking about the Kaiser. They'd said that the German Emperor was building up his fleet of warships. 'Ready to attack our Navy!' one of the boys had said. But apart from that he had no real idea what the spectators were talking about.

He knew, though, that Annie Oakley never missed her target, whatever she shot at. She seemed to have eyes like a cat.

All too soon, the show reached its finale. Buffalo

Bill made one last gallop around the arena. Just like Annie Oakley, he was shooting coloured glass balls thrown up into the air by a young Indian boy. The difference this time was that he did it from horseback. But, like Annie, he never missed his target.

And then it was over. With the smell of gunpowder still lingering in his nostrils, Sam joined the thousands of others who were filing out into the late afternoon sunshine. His mind was whirling with the excitement and the energy of it all.

The smell of cooking was beginning to waft from the direction of the Indian camp and Sam realised that he was hungry. It was time to forget the fantasy of the Wild West show and start thinking about practicalities. He needed to find food and shelter for the night. That would not be easy. It never was. But it had to be done and nothing could ever take away the magic of those wonderful few hours spent watching the show.

Chapter Three

MURDER

It was a long, cold night. Sam found nothing to eat apart from a couple of stale sandwiches he scavenged at the back of one of the cafés in Queen Street. And so he set off to tramp the streets to find his friends.

As he walked, he thought about Running Water and the people in the Wild West show, all under the watchful eye of Buffalo Bill Cody. Like one big family, Sam thought. His own parents had died so long ago that he really did not miss them. Sometimes he thought of his mother as he was drifting off to sleep, but when he woke the vision had always disappeared.

After his parents' death he'd spent a short time in the workhouse and then in an industrial school, where orphans and neglected children were sent to be looked after. Looked after? All Sam could remember were the grim surroundings, the harsh discipline and the poor food. Pretty soon, he'd run away.

But he was young and didn't know much about living rough. The only way he could get food was to steal it from the stalls and barrows on the market, putting himself at risk every time he reached out to grab a loaf of bread or a hunk of cheese.

Before long, the police had picked him up.

'You should be in school,' the sergeant had told him. 'We've got just the place for runaways like you.'

This time they sent him to a truant school, a place called Bryn y Don in Dinas Powys, miles away from Cardiff, right out in the country. But, if the industrial school had been rough and tough, Bryn y Don was ten times worse. A fist across the back of the head was the standard punishment, a beating with the birch rod for more serious offences, and the days were long and hard, working at manual tasks like mending shoes and sewing mail sacks. They called the place a school but as far as Sam could see there didn't seem to be very much education on offer. It didn't take him long to decide what he was going to do.

'I can't stand it here,' he hissed to one of the other lads, a pale, quiet boy called Paul. 'I'm off, first chance I get. You coming?'

The other boy agreed and, one night, when the lights had been turned out, they saw their chance, slipped out through a side door when one of the warders went out for a smoke, and struggled over the back wall under cover of darkness. It was harder than Sam expected. Paul was younger than he was and hardly had enough energy to climb the wall before he was racked by a fit of coughing. Sam had to catch hold of him to stop him from sliding down and then pull him up and over the sharp stones at the top. Sam was surprised at how little his new friend weighed. He was shocked by the boniness of his thin body as they landed awkwardly on the other side.

They didn't know each other well – no one got close at Bryn y Don because regulations meant that the boys were forbidden to talk – but Sam could see how ill he was. He needed to be in the infirmary, not out in the night air, running away.

'Thanks for taking me with you,' whispered Paul as they stumbled along the road edge in the dark, looking fearfully behind them.

Even at that time of night Sam could see how waxy pale he was and he thought maybe he should try and get his friend to a hospital. He dismissed the idea almost immediately. The doctors and nurses would only send them back to Bryn y Don and Paul would get no help there. And so they limped along, stopping regularly to let Paul recover his breath.

'I'm holding you up,' he wheezed, his words almost lost in a fit of coughing. 'Leave me and go on.'

Sam shook his head. 'We ran away together; we stay together.'

Paul smiled at him gratefully, and they staggered on. Just after midnight the wind got up and it began to rain. Their thin shirts were no protection and within minutes they were soaked. Sam knew they had to find shelter.

At last they found an empty barn. It was old and draughty but at least it was somewhere to rest.

'Thanks, Sam,' Paul gasped. 'Sorry I'm slowing you down. It's kind of you to help me – anyone else would have left me long ago.' He lay down on the floor and Sam found an old piece of sacking to put over him. Soon Paul drifted off into a restless sleep.

Morning found him shivering uncontrollably. Sam stared at the beads of perspiration across his forehead. He was clearly running a fever and, for the first time, Sam was really frightened for his friend. 'I'll go and find us something to eat,' he said. 'You stay here.'

Paul gazed at him with unseeing eyes. Already he seemed to be far away and, for a moment, Sam wondered if the sick boy thought he was running away from him. But he had to go and find food.

When he came back, he tried to wake Paul but there was no response.

What if he was dead? Sam felt the panic in his belly swelling, overtaking every other emotion. 'They'll blame me,' he thought. 'They'll say it was my fault, that I killed him. Then no one will be able to put the blame on the matron or the superintendent.' Sam knew he couldn't stay where he was and he couldn't leave Paul either. He had the idea that if he could find somewhere safe for him, there might just be a chance. He could see, by the faint rise and fall beneath his shirt, that the boy was still alive – just. He'd get him to the church porch and leave him there for someone to find, then he'd wait till dark and make his way back to the city. The police mustn't catch him or he'd be in terrible trouble.

*

And so began Sam's new life, living on the streets of Cardiff once again, avoiding the police, living on his wits, learning to run at the first sign of danger.

It wasn't such a bad existence. This time he made friends with others like himself who hung around the docks and railway station. They'd protected him until such time as he was able to take care of himself. Now they treated him as an equal. They all looked out for each other, and tried to share whatever they might find. Together, they ran from the police and, if they were lucky, earned a few pennies carrying bags, running errands or, in the winter, shovelling leaves or snow from the pavements.

Tonight, though, he seemed to be alone on the streets of Cardiff. He tried all the usual haunts but there was no sign of anyone he knew. 'Where is everybody?' he wondered. 'Perhaps the police did a sweep after the Wild West show and picked them all up. Picked up everyone but me.'

Sam was used to being alone but this night there seemed to be a silence about the city that set his heart pounding. He jumped at every sudden shadow and found himself startled by stalking cats or scuttling rats.

At last he saw a faint glimmer of light in the eastern

sky and he heard the clock on St John's Church strike five as he turned into the Hayes. It was the second or third time he had been in the square that night and he quickly moved on, making for Bute Street and the docks area. He knew that if he could get past the policeman on the gates there might well be the chance of food and something to drink from some generous sailor or dock worker.

But before he reached the far end of Caroline Street, he changed his mind and thought that perhaps he would try his luck at the railway station. 'Maybe there'll be some early travellers who'll want a hand with their luggage,' he told himself and pushed his cold hands deeper into his trouser pockets.

Head bowed, he almost ran full tilt into the back of a tall man standing in the shadows halfway down the street. Sam pulled back into the deep shelter of a shop doorway, afraid the man might have seen him.

The street was poorly lit but, even so, in the light of the man's glowing cigarette, Sam could see that his hair was jet black and, in his right hand, he was carrying a heavy canvas sack.

As Sam watched, another figure joined the stranger. To his amazement, he recognized Mr Tomkins, the sweet-shop owner.

'Where the devil have you been?' demanded the unknown man, his words hissing out like escaping gas. 'It's nearly morning; people are going to be up and about soon.'

Mr Tomkins spread his hands wide and smirked, a calculating grin that had no warmth in it. 'There's time enough yet. I had to get the money from my shop.'

The other man shook his head and sighed. Sam sensed that he was angry at being kept waiting, angry and anxious that they might be disturbed. Yet his greed was clearly stronger than any other emotion. 'No matter. You're here now. Where's the money?'

Tomkins held up a black leather bag, exactly like the travelling cases doctors used to tend to their patients.

'All here, as you asked, two hundred pounds. And you've got the goods?'

The dark man held out his sack and Tomkins passed across the bag. There was a momentary flash of light as the dark man tossed his dying cigarette butt into the gutter, the stub arching through the air. The man tucked the bag under his arm and turned on his heel to go.

'Wait,' called Tomkins. 'I want to check the bag.'

'There's no need for that,' said the man, quickly. 'Everything's there, as we agreed.'

There was alarm in his voice and, instinctively, Sam knew that he was lying. Perhaps Mr Tomkins picked up the same feeling. He bent over the canvas bag and began to pull at the drawstring that held its neck. 'Always check the goods,' he said, speaking into the darkness. 'That's the first rule of business.' He reached into the bag and began to rummage about amongst the contents.

'Hold on,' he said after a moment. 'This isn't what you promised me. There's nothing here but old stones and paper.' Tomkins threw down the bag and stood up. He moved closer to the other man and reached out to grab him by the front of his coat.

'You're a cheat, man, a good-for-nothing cheat. You really expect me to pay two hundred pounds for that heap of rubbish?'

They were the last words he ever spoke. A knife blade flashed and, with a deep sigh, Mr Tomkins fell forward onto the cobblestones. A wide circle of blood began to form around his head and Sam knew that he must be dead.

'No,' he gasped into the darkness. 'Oh, no.'

His words were no more than a whisper but they were enough to tell the killer that he was not alone. The dark man spun around and his eyes seemed to bore into Sam.

'You killed him,' Sam stuttered, slowly backing away. 'You killed him.'

The man held up his blood-stained knife, pointing it at Sam's throat. 'Yes. And I'll kill you if you don't stay where you are.'

His voice was harsh though surprisingly light for such a big man, but Sam had eyes only for the long Bowie knife, and he carried on backing away until he felt the rough stone wall behind his shoulders.

'Just business, boy,' said the man, inching closer. 'He was trying to cheat me; there was nothing else I could do.'

Sam knew the man was lying because of the way he held the leather grip tightly to his side, ignoring the worthless canvas bag alongside Mr Tomkins's body. It was all the proof Sam needed. 'Him cheating you?' he whispered. 'I thought it was the other way around. So what did he say was in the canvas bag? Stones? Paper?'

The dark man shrugged. The boy was clearly streetwise. He grinned and the smile made him seem even crueller.

'What did he think he was buying?' asked Sam.

'You don't need to know, boy. Let's just say he thought he was getting the bargain of the century. Now he's dead and I've got his money, lots and lots of lovely money. And do you know something? He's not getting it back.'

Sam had little love for Mr Tomkins. The man had cuffed him around the ear and cursed him too often. But nobody deserved to die like that, in the street. The image of his friend Paul suddenly swam into Sam's brain. What if he too had died? He shook his head to clear it of the picture.

'You don't agree with me?' said the dark man. 'Well, that's just too bad.' He turned and spat, carelessly, in the direction of the body. It was a brief movement, a momentary lapse of concentration, but it gave Sam the chance he needed. He took to his heels and ran.

'Boy!' he heard the man roar. 'Get back here, now!'

Sam sped on, down Caroline Street and out into the Hayes. The clatter of hobnailed boots on the road behind him told him that the stranger was following, chasing him hard. Sam was fast, at least over a short distance, but his pursuer, powered by fear of discovery, was just as fast. And, as the great bulk of Cardiff Castle appeared in front of him, Sam realised that the man was gaining ground.

There was no movement in the silent city, apart from the flickering shadows of the two runners. And soon, Sam, whose burst of speed couldn't last, was panting with weakness and exhaustion.

He glanced behind him. The killer was closer now. Where could Sam run? In the next instant he'd made it across the Taff river bridge and the tall trees of Sophia Gardens were flashing past. The Indian village was silent and still, the tepees shuttered up and empty. Sam remembered the words of Running Water – the show people slept in the covered wagons, she had said. But perhaps the tents might give him a hiding place.

The first two tepees were securely tied and he lost valuable moments trying to untie the leather strings that held the doorways together. The pounding of feet and the panting of breath in the early morning air told him that his pursuer was now very close.

And then, when he had almost given up hope, he heard a voice. 'Sam, in here. Quick!'

He swung round. Running Water was standing at the door of her tepee, two large buckets of water at her side. 'Come on,' she said, beckoning him in.

Sam dived through the half-open doorway and threw himself to the ground while Running Water quickly fastened the entrance behind them.

'Not a sound,' said the girl. 'Just watch.'

They lay on the braided rugs and Running Water reached out to raise the bottom of the tent by an inch or so. Within seconds they saw the legs of the dark man come into view. Sam and Running Water craned their necks but no matter how hard they tried, they could see no higher than the killer's knees.

The man came to a halt in front of the tent. For a moment it seemed as if he had guessed where Sam was hiding. But why had he simply stopped? Inside the tepee, Sam was puzzled. The man must know where he'd gone. What was he waiting for?

Suddenly there was movement and Sam held his breath. But, to his amazement, came the sound of retreating footsteps. Clearly the man was moving away.

'So what was all that about?' asked Running Water when the man had finally gone. 'Did you steal his wallet?'

Sam told her briefly what had happened, how he had witnessed the murder and been chased. The girl listened patiently, nodding in places, staring open-mouthed in others. 'And you knew this man?' she asked when Sam had finished his tale. 'I mean, the man who was stabbed?'

'Yes,' Sam nodded. 'He owned a shop in St Mary Street. The other one, the killer, I've never seen him before.'

Running Water rolled over onto her back and stared up at the sloping roof and sides of the tepee. 'It's lucky for you I was out fetching water. Otherwise he'd have caught you for sure.'

Sam knew she spoke the truth – it was not something he cared to think about too much. But at least now the man had gone and the question of what to do next began to loom large in his mind.

'You could go to the police,' suggested Running Water.

Sam grinned at her words. 'The coppers? They wouldn't believe a word I said. They hate all of us street boys – they'd lock us up and throw away the key if they could. Every time they catch one of us they whip us into court and next thing we know we get sent off to one of the reformatory schools. And besides, I can't go to the police. There's reasons. They're complicated – you wouldn't understand.'

'All right,' said Running Water. 'But school – what did you call them, reformatory schools? They can't be that bad.'

Sam shrugged. 'You want to bet? I tried it once,

a truant school, just the same as a reformatory. You don't need school to stay alive on the streets. So, no, I'm not going anywhere near the police. And, besides, I don't know who the man is. How could I identify him? This is a port. People are coming and going all the time – there must be dozens of sailors around the docks who look like him. He'll probably be off to India or Japan or somewhere before the day's out.'

He stopped and ran his hands through his hair, then glanced across at the Indian girl. 'They'll find the body soon enough. It'll be just another unsolved crime as far as the police are concerned.'

'I suppose you're right,' said Running Water. 'The most important thing is to keep you safe. If the murderer finds you he'll do the same to you as he did to your Mr Tomkins. You've got to lie low for a while.'

Sam knew the girl was making sense but something deep inside told him that Mr Tomkins deserved a better justice than this – no matter how unpleasant he had been. 'I hate to think the killer will get away with it – murder and robbery – whoever he is.'

The girl shrugged. 'You can't do anything about it. You can't catch the killer and you can't help Mr Tomkins. He's dead, beyond worrying. Stay safe, Sam, stay out of the way of that man.'

'I will but it doesn't make it right. He killed a man.'

'He'll get his comeuppance sometime. Just wait a while.'

He knew Running Water spoke the truth. He had

to stay out of the killer's way, at least for a time. He had to get out of the city.

The girl was already ahead of him. 'There's nothing else for it; you'd better stay here, with us, in the Wild West show. We're leaving Cardiff later today, pulling out, so you can easily join the show – you can become one of us.'

Sam shook his head. She made it sound so simple. 'I can't do that. People will know I don't belong. Who's going to let me join the Wild West show? I'm just a street boy from Cardiff.'

Running Water laughed, her eyes sparkling in the darkness of the tepee. 'Believe me, Sam, there's no folk like the show people we've got here. You leave it to me – I'll see to everything.'

Chapter Four

SAM SPEED

Sam was expecting problems and delay – fierce arguments between Running Water and her family at the very least – but he was amazed at how quickly and efficiently everything was arranged.

He and Running Water crept carefully out of the tepee, making sure that the killer was nowhere in sight, and made their way to the covered wagon where the girl lived with her mother.

'My father was killed some time ago,' she explained as they walked, 'fighting against the white men. It was sad – he'd survived Little Bighorn and lots of other battles against the soldiers. And then he got himself shot by some gold prospectors a few years after I was born.' Running Water spoke quickly, as if saying them faster would make her words sound more matter of fact.

When they arrived at the wagon Sam stood outside while Running Water disappeared inside the canvas covering. He closed his eyes, leaning back against the wooden wheel. He felt so tired; all the fear and energy that had kept him going for the past few hours had slipped away. He heard the gentle mumble of voices coming from the inside and then, he supposed, he must have slept where he stood, propped up against the wagon.

He woke with a start. A short, plump woman, an older version of Running Water, was standing in front of him. She had her hands on her hips and Sam knew she was not used to being disobeyed.

'This is my mother,' said Running Water. 'I've told her everything.'

'My name is Star,' said the woman, studying him closely.

'Star what?' asked Sam. 'Don't you have another name?'

The woman shook her head. 'Just Star,' she said. 'I listened to what my daughter had to say. I have no problem with you staying here. We must keep you safe. But first we need to go and see Bill.'

'Bill?' said the astonished Sam. 'You mean Buffalo Bill?'

Star nodded. 'He is wise in these things. He will advise us. Come.'

She led the way across the village to where a large wagon, far grander and better painted than any of the others, stood in splendid isolation.

'Bill's wagon,' whispered Running Water.

Buffalo Bill was sitting on a wooden chair, his back to the wagon, cleaning his rifle. Two of the rough-riders from the show were lounging at the tailboard, playing a game with dice and cards. A few feet away sat a slim woman dressed in buckskins. With a start, Sam realised that it was Annie Oakley.

'Well,' drawled Bill, looking up at the newcomers, 'what in tarnation do we have here?' With his booted foot he pushed across a small wooden bench. He nodded at the bench and indicated that they should sit. 'Stay a while and take the weight off your feet. Star, you know who everyone is but, for our guest,' – he nodded at Sam – 'this is my very particular friend, Miss Annie Oakley.'

Sam gulped while Bill continued: 'You may have heard about her, son. Next to me she's the greatest shot in the world.'

Annie Oakley was dark-haired and very pretty, Sam decided. He raised his hand in a half wave. Annie smiled at him, and then turned to Buffalo Bill. 'Oh, I reckon I'm a whole lot better than that, Bill. Better than you, I guess. Maybe one day we'll find a way to prove it.'

Annie turned back to face Sam and stuck out her hand. 'Howdy, youngster. What can Bill and I do for you today?'

Sam opened his mouth to speak but, to his amazement, no words came out. He sat there, mouth working like a goldfish, but totally mute until Annie Oakley finally came to his rescue.

'I guess he's a little overawed,' she said. 'Maybe you'd better help him out, Star.'

Star nodded and, between them, she and Running Water told the story of Sam's adventure. Buffalo Bill and Annie sat listening intently. Only when the tale had been told did Bill finally turn towards Sam.

'So, son, can you describe this man? What did he look like?'

Sam nodded. He felt the anger and disgust rise in his chest – oh yes, he could describe the man right enough. And this time he did manage to find his voice. 'He was tall and big, big as you, sir. He had black hair. And he can run really fast.'

Despite the seriousness of the situation, Buffalo Bill and Annie laughed out loud. Annie sat forward in her chair. 'I guess he can – if he can outpace you.'

Bill cut her off with a wave of his hand. 'He sounds like a very dangerous man indeed,' he said. 'I wonder what he was trying to sell – or, perhaps I should say, pretending to sell?'

'Did this Mr Tomkins say what it was he was buying?' asked Annie.

Sam shook his head. 'He never said anything much. He didn't get the chance. But it must have been valuable – he was going to pay a lot of money for it.'

He felt Running Water go suddenly tense at his side. She shuddered. 'All he got for it was a knife in the neck.'

'Quickest way to kill a man,' said Bill. 'It's an old Indian trick. Sorry, my dear, but it's true. I've seen lots of men killed that way.'

There was silence for a few moments before Bill spoke again. 'Sam, I think it's pretty clear that Running Water and Star are right. We've got to keep you safe. I wouldn't fancy your chances if you happened to meet this character again so I reckon you're safer here with us – a lot safer than roaming the streets of Cardiff every night. He'll be out there looking for you, you can bet on that. So, do you fancy joining the Wild West show for a while?'

Sam could hardly believe Bill's words. But he nodded, eagerly. There was nothing he would like more.

Buffalo Bill studied him for a few moments. 'Your face and arms are pretty dark and sunburned – seems like even here in Wales you get a little warm weather now and then. Star, get some stain on his chest and back and I reckon he could pass for an Indian any day.'

Star nodded. 'I will. But first he needs a bath. The smell round here ain't none too good since he arrived.'

Everyone laughed, apart from Sam. The thought of bathing had little appeal for him. Star took him by the arm and led him away. When he glanced back he saw that Bill and Annie were leaning close together, obviously in deep and serious conversation.

*

The wagons of the Wild West show left Cardiff that afternoon, rolling in a long caravan through the city streets, heading north into the mining valleys of south Wales. The harnesses of the horses jangled, the wagons rolled from side to side in an easy rhythm, and Sam supposed that the people who stood, enthralled, watching them as they jogged past, had never seen anything so exotic.

'I expect, for them, it's like Christmas and the Sunday-School treat rolled into one,' he told Running Water.

'What's a Sunday-School treat?' the girl asked.

'A trip to the seaside. Once a year the churches and chapels run them for people who go to their Sunday School.'

'That must be fun,' said Running Water.

Sam shrugged. 'I don't know. I've never been on one.'

He sat next to Running Water in the back of the wagon and watched as the streets of Cardiff were left behind. Within a few miles the mining valleys began and soon the terraced houses and coal mines came into view.

Apart from his time at the truant school, Sam had never been out of Cardiff. The long ribbons of houses and the steep-sided valleys were as strange to him as they were to Running Water. All day they trundled northwards, crossing sluggish rivers, black with the dust and grime of coal pits, and running along narrow roadways that seemed to be nailed to the hillsides.

There were two other youngsters travelling with them, a boy and a girl. Running Water introduced them as Tommy Two Moons and Summer Storm.

'Is all of Wales like this?' asked Tommy, pointing at the black heaps of mining waste and the colliery winding gear. 'Don't you have any plains or lakes or real mountains?'

'There's just no room to breathe,' said Summer. 'Everyone is living on top of one another.'

Sam looked at his new friends. 'They say there's lots of hills and mountains to the north and west. But I've never seen them. Not yet.'

'Maybe you will on this trip,' smiled Summer.

They fell silent, gazing out at the blackened landscapes but, inside, Sam was smiling to himself. He'd started to relax, and as they got further and further from the town, he began to enjoy the trip. It was like a new start in life, he decided. Cardiff and the streets were behind him – perhaps this was the beginning of something new, something really good for a change.

True to her word, as soon as they had left Buffalo Bill earlier in the day, Star had filled a huge tub with boiling water. 'You've got a choice,' she said, looking pointedly at Sam's tattered clothes. 'Either you take those rags off, or I do!'

Sam assured her he was quite capable of bathing

himself, if she'd only turn her back. To his relief, Star busied herself with pots and pans whilst he took refuge in the steaming water. Soon he was cleaner than he'd been for several years. And afterwards, dressed in new, tight-fitting buckskin trousers and shirt, Sam Thomas looked for all the world like a young Indian brave.

'We'll have to give you an Indian name,' Star announced. 'I've heard of Indians called Sam but never Sam Thomas. What do you think, Running Water?'

The girl had stared at him, marvelling at the change in his appearance. 'I think we should keep the name Sam,' she said at last. 'We might forget and give the game away if we called him anything else. What about Sam Speed? After all, I know how fast he can run.'

*

And so it was decided. When he had taken his place in the wagon that afternoon he was simply introduced as Sam Speed, a new addition to the show. Tommy and Summer had asked no questions about the mysterious stranger who'd suddenly appeared in their midst and just accepted him as a new friend.

'Don't worry about them,' Running Water had whispered. 'They know not to ask too many questions. They're friends. That's all that matters. Their parents look after the ponies and the buffalo – they've got to herd them from one place to the next. That's why they ride with us.'

They camped that night on a wide and open field in Porth, the gateway to the Rhondda Valley. There were fires to build and water to be fetched but as soon as the jobs were done, Running Water and Sam Speed slipped away. They found a quiet spot on the riverbank and, as the long shadows of evening crept in towards them, they sat and spoke about all that had happened.

'I don't know what other people would feel,' Sam said, 'but, despite what happened to Mr Tomkins, I think I'm happy.'

Running Water shrugged. 'Good. It'll work out, Sam. We've got Bill and Annie on our side and that's great. Both of them, they're dead straight.'

Sam stared at her, not understanding.

'I mean,' she continued, 'that they're honest. They care. Look at the way they treat us Indians. Most white men in our country aren't interested in what happens to us. They put us into reservations and . . .'

'Reservations?' interrupted Sam.

'Like big camps – prisons without the wire and walls. There's nothing to do there, no buffalo to hunt, no prairies to roam. So the men, the braves, get drunk on cheap whisky. Then they quarrel and fight each other. They're terrible places, Sam, run by people who hate us.' She paused and stared out across the river. Carelessly, she picked up a pebble and tossed it into the water. 'Sometimes I think that everyone hates us. All the Indian wars you've heard about – Custer and the rest – they only happened because the white men were greedy. They found gold on our territories and we were in the way. Then they wanted our hunting lands to farm, to raise cattle – we were in the way again.'

'That's not what we're told over here,' said Sam. 'All we hear about are bloodthirsty Indians killing white settlers, taking scalps and all that.'

Running Water shook her head. 'Scalping? The white men started that, not us. They put a price on our heads and the only way the hunters could prove they'd killed so many Indians was to take their scalps.'

Sam shuddered at the thought of it. 'I never knew,' he said.

The girl turned towards him, spreading her arms wide. 'Not many people do. Like I said, everyone hates us. But not Bill. He cares about the Indians, about what happens to us. Oh, he fought us all right, killed hundreds of our warriors in his time. That was his job, what he was paid to do. But he respects us and helps us keep our traditions alive.'

'Is that what this Wild West show is really all about, then?' asked Sam. 'Keeping alive all the old traditions?'

Running Water thought for a moment. 'Maybe. Perhaps a little bit. But Bill's a clever businessman who knows how to make money. There's nothing wrong in showing us off to the world, is there?'

She didn't need an answer. Already they were firm friends who didn't feel the need to talk if there was nothing to say.

Presently, they heard Star calling that supper was ready and they made their way back to the camp. Dusk had fallen and the sharp yellow glow of two dozen cooking fires winked through the gloom.

Chapter Five

HEADING WEST

Over the next few weeks the Wild West show made slow but steady progress through the valleys of south-east Wales, making their way gradually westwards towards Bridgend and Neath, attracting crowds of thousands wherever they went.

Sam had never seen or felt excitement like it. In every town or village it was the same, the air full of tension and expectation. You could almost touch it, he thought, knowing that for the thousands who came to watch and stare as the wagon train trundled into town, this was the highlight of their year. And now he was part of it.

In the evenings he sat with Star and Running Water and tried to pick up some of the learning that the Indian woman was giving her daughter. 'We must teach you to read, Sam,' she said. 'You won't get far in life without that.'

And slowly, as the days went past, he began to pick it up. He took great delight in working out what the shapes and letters actually meant though at first they'd danced in front of his eyes. Sometimes Star would sit beside him at the fire and, as the evening closed in around the showground, tell him stories about her tribe, spellbinding tales of famous battles and of hunting for buffalo on the Great Plains. He would have given anything to visit those Indian hunting grounds. One day, he told himself, one day he'd go there.

In the meantime he had the Wild West show. It was a huge adventure, a miracle of organisation. Just the practicalities of moving so many people each day, travelling from one town to the next, was something that intrigued Sam. 'Who arranges all this?' he asked one day as the wagons jolted onto the showground at Swansea. 'I mean, who works out where we stay and perform?'

'Bill arranged most of it before we left America,' said Summer Storm. 'But he's got an advance manager who goes on ahead of us, making sure everything is ready for us when we arrive. He's called Morgan Stanfield.'

'Morgan Stanfield?' echoed Sam. 'I've never seen him.'

'You're not the only one,' said Running Water. 'I've been here the whole trip and I haven't seen him either.'

'You won't,' said Tommy Two Moons. 'He's always a couple of days ahead of us. The only time you're likely to come across him is if we spend two or three days in the same place – like we did in

Cardiff, like we're going to do in Pembroke Dock next month.'

'Probably just as well,' said Summer, shaking her head. 'He's not the nicest of people to know. He hates all us Indians so we try to stay out of his way as much as we can.'

They began to unpack the wagon and set up camp. As he worked, Sam thought back over the last couple of weeks. To begin with he had stayed in the background, sitting outside the tepee with the others but taking no part in the show itself. Gradually, however, as he became more confident, he began to sit alongside Running Water in the wagon for the opening parade. And, surprisingly, he soon found that he was beginning to enjoy the experience.

Then, only yesterday, Buffalo Bill had approached him as he was walking back to the wagon train. The showman had a huge smile on his handsome, ruddy face. 'Howdy, son. Enjoying being part of the show?'

Sam nodded eagerly.

Bill clapped him on the shoulder. 'Good. And no sign of our murderer? He hasn't reappeared?'

For a moment Sam thought Bill was laughing at him. Then he saw the serious glint in the man's eyes and the horror of that night in Cardiff came sweeping back. 'No, sir. I guess I'd all but forgotten about him – until you just reminded me.'

Bill fell into step alongside him. 'Don't ever forget him, Sam. He's out there somewhere and one of these days maybe he'll reappear. Put him to the back of your mind but never forget who he is or what he did. He'll get caught soon enough, you mark my words.'

They stopped outside Star's wagon. 'But that's not what I wanted to talk about with you. You've been with us long enough now and you've seen how the show works. Most important, you've seen how we end each performance.'

'With you charging around the showground,' said Sam, 'shooting those glass balls out of the air.' He had watched it every day, marvelling at Bill's accuracy with his six-shooters.

Bill nodded. 'Well, every performance I use a different boy to throw the balls up into the air. I reckon it's about time you had a go. What do you think?'

Sam stared at the man, amazed that he was offering him this chance. 'Really? You're serious? You really want me to throw up the balls? Do you think I can do it?'

'Sure,' said Bill. 'There's nothing to it. You throw them up, I shoot them down. OK, son, we'll do it tomorrow, in the Swansea show.' He winked at Sam and strode off towards his wagon.

Sam was excited and happy but, as the day wore on, he began to have doubts. 'Suppose I can't do it properly?' he said to Running Water that night. 'What if I make Bill miss? He'll look like a fool – and it'll be my fault.'

50

Running Water laughed and nudged him playfully in the ribs. 'He won't miss. He never does. You know those guns he uses, his Colt 45s? Well, he's had them specially made. They don't shoot bullets; they shoot lots of little pellets, like a shotgun. When the guns fire, the pellets spray out all over the place. There's hundreds of them. The crowd can't see them, of course. He couldn't miss, even if he wanted to.'

Sam was shocked and he stared at Running Water with dismay. 'Do you mean he cheats? Every time he goes into the show he's cheating – is that what you're saying?'

'Not really,' said the girl. 'He's just giving the crowd what they want. They want him to shatter those glass balls – and so he does.' She stood up and walked to the edge of the showring, then called back over her shoulder to Sam. 'And besides, have you ever tried to pick up one of those 45s? They're so heavy you wouldn't be able to hold them up for more than a couple of seconds – let alone fire at a tiny glass ball from the back of a galloping horse. It's all part of the show.'

Sam knew she was right and they left it at that. But now they had arrived in Swansea and his great moment was almost on him.

The following afternoon, once the parade had passed by, once the re-enactments had taken place and Annie Oakley had amazed the crowd with her sharp shooting, Sam made his way to the corral at the back of the showground. Buffalo Bill was waiting for him. From inside the ground came the thundering of hooves and the wild shrieks and cries of the Indian war band. Moments later, the riders came bounding out of the ring. It was almost time.

'Ready?' asked Bill.

'As ready as I'll ever be,' Sam said, the nerves in his belly dancing around like butterflies.

He gathered up his bag of coloured glass balls and inched towards the showring. He had barely reached the entrance when, to a roar of approval from the crowd, Buffalo Bill charged past him, his white horse kicking up huge clods of earth and dust.

Once, twice, three times, Bill rode around the circle of spectators, then reined in his horse. The animal, experienced and clever as Bill himself, shied up on his hind legs and Bill waved his hat in the air. 'Time for a little fine shooting, folks,' he declared.

The crowd roared again and Sam suddenly felt a presence behind him. He turned to see Annie Oakley smiling at him. 'Go on, Sam, that's your cue.' She pushed him gently into the showring. Sam took up a position halfway down the arena, as he had seen other boys do. He stared at Buffalo Bill, trying to ignore the combined gaze of several thousand spectators. A tense hush descended over the entire ground.

'Let's go!' Bill shouted and came charging towards him.

For a moment Sam froze, a glass ball glued to his sweaty palm.

'Throw it!' hissed Annie from the wings.

That was the trigger. Sam threw the ball high into the air. An instant later there was a deafening explosion as Bill's Colt roared and the ball exploded into a million tiny pieces.

The applause from the crowd was like a thunderstorm directly overhead. 'Again!' called Annie, once the noise had subsided and Bill was once more circling the ring.

The colour, the smell of the sawdust, the smoke and the roar of the crowd would stay with Sam for the rest of his life. No matter how often he appeared in the show, nothing would ever come close to that first time. For nearly ten minutes he stood there, hurling the glass globes into the air, sometimes as many as three or four at a time.

Mischievously, he tried to catch Bill out, throwing the balls when he wasn't looking, but the roar of the crowd always alerted the cowboy. He would whirl around, his guns would crack and another couple of balls would shatter.

When his bag was finally empty, Sam turned it inside out to show the spectators that the exhibition was over and then he bowed briefly before slipping quickly from the arena and leaving Bill to take his final bow.

A few moments later, Buffalo Bill joined him

backstage. 'Nice throwing, Sam,' he grinned. 'But you'll have to get up earlier in the day if you want to catch me out like that.'

'It worked really well,' said Annie, putting her arm around Sam's shoulders. 'Perhaps you should keep Sam in the act.'

Bill nodded and stroked his beard. 'Maybe,' he said. 'Maybe I will.'

*

From Swansea, the Wild West show headed towards Carmarthen and now, at last, Tommy and Summer were able to see a different side to Wales. 'It's really beautiful,' Summer exclaimed, 'all so green and rich.'

Sam pretended not to be interested but, inside, he was as thrilled as his friends. He had never seen anything as lovely as this part of Wales and was secretly amazed at the contrasts to be found within such a small country. The rolling green hills and the wide valleys, the tiny cottages with smoke rising from their chimneys – it was a whole world away from the blackness of the mining valleys to the east.

Another day, another show, with Sam again throwing the balls for Buffalo Bill – and more ecstatic applause before they rolled, once more, out of town. This time they were heading to the far west of the country.

They arrived in Pembroke Dock late on a Monday afternoon. Bill had gone on ahead to meet Morgan Stanfield, Annie said, taking the train from Carmarthen. Now, when the show finally arrived, he was waiting for them at the entrance to the ground where they would both camp and perform.

'Straight ahead,' he called, waving the wagons through the gate. 'Let's get you all settled in before it's dark.'

Sam was an old hand at it now and setting up camp was quickly and easily done. Within half an hour the tepees were erected, the wagons corralled for the night and the campfires lit.

'We're going to have a look at the town,' Running Water called.

'One hour, no more,' warned Star.

They waved happily and set off. The showground was on the edge of the town and it took them some minutes to walk into the centre. Running Water was amazed. She had never expected to find such wide and elegant streets. 'Not even Cardiff has streets as wide as this,' she exclaimed. 'I've seen the roads in Chicago and St Louis – even they'd be hard pushed to beat these.'

Sam had never seen Chicago or St Louis but he knew the girl was right about the elegance of this road system. They were standing at a crossroads in the middle of the town. To their right lay a street full of shops and businesses while the road ahead seemed to be made up of tall, elegant houses. From their left came the panting of a steam engine – clearly the town railway station lay in that direction.

Sam had heard Bill and Annie talking about Pembroke Dock and thought he knew the reason for the wide streets. 'This is a dockyard town,' he told Running Water. 'This is the place where they build all the ships for the Royal Navy. And this was where they produced the royal yachts for the old Queen – well, the new King, too, I suppose. The roads have to be wide to let the wagons pass, the wagons that carry all the wood and steel to build the ships.'

Running Water grunted. She was staring at an elegantly dressed woman who had just walked past, her nose in the air and a green parasol shading her from a sun that had long since disappeared for the night. She was the third or fourth person they had passed and it had been the same every time. Sam would have expected Running Water and himself to attract attention, two strange and exotic children dressed in colourful buckskin outfits. But none of the passers-by even gave them a second glance.

'I guess it's an important place,' said the girl. 'But I do think these people are pretty full of themselves. They seem to think that they're special, just because their dockyard built a few ships for old Queen Victoria.'

They turned and walked slowly back to the showground. Half a mile to the west, Sam could see the tall shapes of sheer legs and giant building sheds.

They lined the water's edge, jutting like broken teeth into the evening sky. Perhaps Running Water was right, he thought, the people here were certainly full of their own self-importance.

But then, this was a famous place. They had built so many great warships for the Navy, some of the greatest ships in the world, everybody said, and maybe the people of the town had a right to be proud.

They had almost reached the wagons and the ring of tepees. From ahead came the low rumble of voices, the clatter of cooking utensils, all the usual sounds of the camp at night. It was warm and it was welcoming – it was, Sam knew, his home. The cooking fires around the wagons glowed red and yellow, guttering gently in the warm breeze that came off the sea. The smell of cooking food wafted towards them and Sam felt saliva gather in his mouth.

'I'm starving,' said Running Water. 'Race you to the wagon.' They broke into a run, charging around the side of the Deadwood Stage where it was parked in the shadows for the night. The dark shape of a man loomed up suddenly in front of them and Sam, head down and panting, had no chance of avoiding him.

'Look out,' the man called.

With a thump that rattled all the teeth in his head, Sam ran full tilt into the dark figure. He cannoned off, staggering backwards with his feet slipping on the dew-soaked grass. Then he fell, full length, onto his back.

'Damned Indian brats!'

Though the words were harsh, the voice was surprisingly light. Sam recognised it instantly. He raised his head and stared into the hard, unfeeling eyes of his worst nightmare – the man who had killed Mr Tomkins.

Chapter Six

MORGAN STANFIELD

Sam lay on the ground, his mind racing furiously. He was in trouble and he knew it. The killer stood above him, his tall muscular frame outlined against the sky. Sam felt his stomach turn over and twist with horror and fear.

'You want to take more care, boy,' said the man, rubbing at the point on his chest where Sam's head had caught him. 'People of your age need to be seen and not heard.' He glared at the prostrate boy and, in that instant, Sam knew that he had been recognized. The man's eyes narrowed. 'Wait a minute,' he muttered, almost to himself. 'You're no Indian. You're that damned boy from Cardiff, the one who . . .'

He left the sentence unfinished. Sam felt the menace of the killer so strongly, it was almost like something he could touch. He squirmed away along the ground. His back came into contact with a wagon wheel and he pulled himself into a sitting position.

'I've been wondering what happened to you, boy,' snarled the man. 'When the police didn't come calling I guessed you'd run, like the scared rat you are. I thought we'd meet again, sooner or later. And to think you've been here in the Wild West show all along.'

From the corner of his eye, Sam could see where Running Water was standing listening to the man's words. Then, in a sudden movement, she flitted swiftly across the grass behind him. She was heading towards Buffalo Bill's wagon and Sam knew that he had to keep the killer talking until help arrived. The alternative was too terrible even to contemplate.

'Who are you?' Sam gasped. 'Where did you come from?' His chest was tight, constricted, and he could barely breathe.

'Who am I?' hissed the man. 'There's no harm in you knowing. You're not going to be able to do anything about it, not where you're going.'

He puffed out his chest and spread his hands. 'The name's Stanfield, Morgan Stanfield.'

Sam gasped.

Morgan Stanfield nodded slowly and grinned. 'Yes, that's right. I see you've heard of me.'

'But you're part of the show. You're one of Buffalo Bill's men.'

'Hardly,' shrugged Stanfield. 'I take his money, do a job for him, but don't ever call me one of Buffalo Bill's men. You wouldn't understand, boy.' He paused and glared up into the night sky. 'There's things between Bill Cody and me that nobody understands.

Not even him. One day there'll be a reckoning. In the meantime I take his money. Not that he pays much. You expect me to make a living on what he gives me? I don't think so.' The man gazed around at the silent wagons. 'You think being part of the famous Wild West show makes any difference to me? Your idea of loyalty and mine are very different, boy.' He brought up his free hand and clipped Sam sharply around the head. The boy cried out in pain.

'Shut up. You'll be getting a lot worse soon enough.' He paused, then leant forward and hissed into Sam's face. 'I was with Bill Cody the first time he came to your godforsaken country all those years ago. We performed for royalty then, for Queen Victoria herself. And all the crowned heads of Europe – the German Kaiser, the lot of them. And I was with him when we came back four years later. Since then we've performed all over America and Bill's made a fortune with his Wild West show – and I'm not a penny richer.' He grinned unpleasantly. 'At least, not as far as Bill Cody is concerned – everyone's entitled to a bit of a sideline. And I've found mine. This place is a goldmine, full of treasures people are only too happy to pay good money for. Selling all those little Indian trinkets and curios, all those painted pictures and medicine-man dolls brings me in a pretty good extra income.'

'But you don't sell anything,' Sam protested. 'You just cheat people out of their money.'

Morgan Stanfield sneered.

Sam felt the man's spittle on his cheek and he shuddered.

'Only sometimes. It all depends how much the customer wants. Your Mr Tomkins, now, he wanted the world – but he was greedy. He deserved what he got.'

Sam felt the anger well up inside him. 'He didn't deserve to get murdered,' he yelled, pulling himself to his feet. 'No one deserves that.'

'Stay there, boy, stay still,' snarled the killer. 'Don't try to run. It'll be easier for you that way.' He moved forward.

And then, out of the darkness, came a voice, hard as steel and cutting through the air like a Bowie knife. 'What's happening here, Morgan.'

Morgan Stanfield spun around. Buffalo Bill and a dozen rough-riders from the show stood glaring at him. Running Water and Annie Oakley, Sam noticed, stood silently to the side.

'Bill,' said Stanfield, suddenly all pleasantness. 'Good to see you again. My little friend and I were just having a quiet chat.'

'Save your wind, Morgan,' said Buffalo Bill. 'We know everything.'

Stanfield stared at him, his eyes shifty, wary and dangerous. 'Everything? What do you mean by that?'

'The murder in Cardiff, for a start. Sam told us

about it, told us what he'd seen, but we didn't know it was you. Not till now.'

'But, Bill, I . . .'

Buffalo Bill cut him short with a sudden wave of his hand. 'Forget it – like I say, the boy's told us everything.'

Annie Oakley moved quickly forward, her arm still draped around Running Water's shoulders. 'We knew things were going missing from the Indian village but we didn't know who was taking them. Not until now.'

Morgan Stanfield shrugged his broad shoulders and smiled at them.

'Stealing is one thing, Morgan,' said Annie. 'Killing? That's something different, something else entirely.'

Stanfield began to inch backwards. 'Oh, come on, Annie. You're not going to take one boy's word against mine? A street boy who probably spends his life stealing and thieving off anybody he can? How long have you known him? A few weeks? You've known me for years. You know I wouldn't do anything like kill a man. The boy's made it all up.'

For a few moments nobody moved or said a word. Everybody seemed to be considering Stanfield's statement. Was it possible? Morgan Stanfield stared directly at Buffalo Bill, his lips curled defiantly. He seemed to be weighing his options. Then he suddenly reached up and pulled a leather bag from his shoulders.

'Look, Bill, I've just got this off the boy. He had

it round his neck.' He leaned forward and tipped out the contents of the bag onto the grass. Knives, beaded shirts and elaborate tomahawks lay in a pile between them.

'See,' said Stanfield. 'He's your thief. He's been taking you all for a ride.'

Bill stared at him, then at Annie Oakley. Stanfield's words seemed to have hit their mark and he seemed suddenly unsure.

'You've forgotten one thing, Morgan,' said Annie.

Stanfield swung around towards her. 'And that is?'

'Running Water. She's been with Sam all evening and she heard you talking to him just now. What do you say, girl? Where does the truth lie?'

Running Water pulled herself up to her full height. She glared at Morgan Stanfield. 'He's lying. Sam never stole anything. Stanfield's the thief – and he's a killer, too. Just now, he admitted it – I heard him.'

Buffalo Bill breathed out easily. He looked relieved and seemed to have made up his mind.

Stanfield stared at him. 'So now you're going to listen to an Indian brat? Good God, Bill, she's as bad as him. They're in this together, can't you see that? She finds the goods in the village, in the wagons; he sells them.'

'Oh, give over, Morgan,' snorted Annie. 'The game's up. You've been caught, red-handed. It's all over.'

Morgan Stanfield stood in front of the crowd of

rough-riders, his face twisted and his mind working furiously. 'You've got no proof, Cody, just their word.' He waved his hand dismissively towards Sam and Running Water. 'It's their word against mine. There's no policeman in the land going to take the word of a couple of brats like that – not against a respectable man like me. But, then, you can believe what you like. I'm not staying here to listen to accusations like these.'

He spun on his heel and began to move away. Then he stopped and turned to face Bill Cody again. 'But seeing as how our partnership seems to have come to an end, maybe I should tell you a few things, a few home truths.'

Sam stared at him. Whatever else Morgan Stanfield might be, he was certainly no coward and he made an impressive figure, standing there in front of Bill Cody and the others.

'I've always hated you, Cody,' Stanfield said, the words spitting out into the night air. 'Right from the moment we first met. Oh, you were so high and mighty, thinking you were doing me such a favour, giving me a job.'

'You don't have to listen to this, Bill,' said Annie.

Cody shook his head. 'No, let him say his piece, Annie. I reckon this has been on his chest for a long while.'

'You're so right,' shouted Stanfield. 'Think back, Bill. Salt Creek Valley in Kansas, just east of Fort Leavenworth, the year 1854. Remember it?'

Bill Cody narrowed his eyes and glared at Stanfield. 'That's where I was raised.'

Stanfield nodded. 'Me, too, except I was ten, maybe twenty years behind you. But my family was there long before you and yours ever appeared on the scene, making a good living homesteading in the valley. Those were the days before the Civil War, before slavery was abolished and so we used black labour. Slaves? They were plentiful – and cheap – and if one died out working the land, we simply bought ourselves another.'

'Slavery!' hissed Annie. 'A filthy, dirty business.'

'You reckon,' said Stanfield, rounding on her. 'That's just what his father thought.' He pointed at Bill Cody, breathing heavily now. 'His father, Isaac Cody – a preacher-man and anti-slavery to the core. Turned the whole valley against us. Before you knew it nobody would speak to us or sell us tools to work the land. Nobody would buy our crops. We were outcasts in our own country, all thanks to his father and his great ideals. We lost the ranch before I was born and I've hated him and his family ever since.'

Cody passed his hand across his forehead and glanced at Annie Oakley. There were tears in his eyes. 'There's bits of truth in what he says. The whole of the valley was for slavery – well Kansas was one of the hotbeds of the slave trade for a long time – until we arrived. My father tried hard to turn them around but it was a difficult road to travel. Lots of fights, lots

66

of arguments, right up until the Civil War broke out. My father died, stabbed in the chest at a political meeting.'

'So his family didn't lose their home because of you?' said Sam.

Cody swung round to stare at him and slowly shook his head. 'No, son, that's just his twisted way of explaining things. They lost the ranch because they were poor farmers. No other reason.'

'Say what you like, Cody,' said Stanfield. 'I know what I know. You offered me this job and I was supposed to be so grateful, like a little puppy. You didn't know it but I hated you and took every chance I could to bring you down. It's one of the reasons I've been ripping you off all these years, taking things from the Indians and selling them.'

'You weren't ripping me off,' said Bill, sadly. 'It was the Indians you were cheating.'

Stanfield sneered. 'Whatever you choose to believe,' he said. 'I'm going now. The air around here has gone a little unpleasant.'

Chapter Seven

ROUGH JUSTICE

Morgan Stanfield smiled at Annie and tipped his hat. Then he turned and began to walk purposefully from the showground.

'Sorry, Morgan,' said Bill, 'but I can't let you go.'

Stanfield swung around, his eyes blazing and fists clenched. 'Stop this nonsense, Cody. I told you, you've got no proof of anything against me.'

Bill Cody said nothing but motioned to the rough-riders. There was a sudden flurry of bodies as they surged forward towards Stanfield. He was outnumbered, twelve to one. But he was a big man and powerful, and he fought like a demon for his freedom. More than one of the rough-riders flew out of the scrum of bodies with head bloodied and teeth missing. Morgan Stanfield was like a man possessed, his feet and fists lashing out time after time. He was fighting, Sam thought, for his very life.

In the end it was sheer weight of numbers that won the day. Stanfield was driven to the ground and held there by the panting rough-riders. Even then his fury and determination to escape gave him an unnatural strength. 'Let me go!' he raged, struggling and spitting at his captors. 'Let me up. I'm warning you, you'll regret this, Cody. I'll make you pay for this.'

'Gag him, for goodness' sake,' said Bill. 'I can't stand any more of his ranting. And tie him well – we don't want him getting loose, at least not anywhile yet.'

By now the whole camp had been roused and a number of the female performers, coats and blankets thrown around their shoulders, had turned out to see what the fuss was about.

Bill turned to speak to them. 'Show's over. Talk to your menfolk; they'll tell you what it's all about.' Then he turned back to the rough-riders and stroked his white beard. 'Now then, we got us a problem. How do we get the cavalry over here? Where's the Sheriff's office in this town?'

'The Sheriff?' whispered Sam. 'This is west Wales, not the Wild West!'

'He means the police,' said Running Water.

'I know where it is,' volunteered Tommy Two Moons, stepping forward. 'The cops have their office over on Charlton Street. I saw it when we were out walking.'

'Will you take my horse and fetch some police over here?' asked Cody.

'Sure thing, Bill.'

'Good kid. Just take care of my horse.'

'Sure, boss,' Tommy grinned, his mind already

fired up by the thought of riding Buffalo Bill's horse. 'You can trust me.'

'I guess so,' said Bill, frowning slightly.

Within minutes Tommy had saddled the white horse and disappeared into the night. Morgan Stanfield now lay, unmoving, on the ground. He was bound hand and foot, the rough-riders taking revenge for their cuts and bruises by pulling the ropes tightly around the man's wrists and ankles. A red neckerchief or bandana was pulled around his mouth.

'Are you all right, Sam?' asked Annie Oakley, sidling up alongside the boy.

She laid her hand on his head and smiled at him. Running Water stood silently on his other side.

Sam felt suddenly hot and tired. But he nodded at his friends. 'I'm fine.'

'Let's go to my wagon,' said Bill. He turned to his men, now standing warily over Morgan Stanfield's prone body. 'Bring him along,' he ordered.

Sam sat alongside Annie outside the ornate wagon. Oil lamps along its side threw out bright semicircles of light, making the night beyond the yellow glow seem even darker. Sam sat with his eyes closed, breathing heavily through his mouth. He knew that Bill and Annie were watching him carefully and when he opened his eyes the first thing he saw was Morgan Stanfield, bound and trussed like a chicken, glaring at him.

'So what happens now?' Sam asked.

Annie leaned forward. 'We turn it over to the police. They can weigh up the evidence. We believe your story but whether the local police do is another matter. As Stanfield said, it's just our word against his. And he comes over as pretty respectable . . . '

'Respectable?' stormed Running Water. 'Respectable?'

'That's what the police would think. Agreed, Bill?'

Buffalo Bill nodded, gravely. 'Sure thing. You said yourself, Sam, that the Cardiff police hate all you street boys. I don't suppose it's much different in this neck of the woods. And they won't trust us show people either.' Then he relaxed and smiled at Sam. 'But maybe British justice will turn up trumps, eh?'

The clatter of horses' hooves brought all of their heads round and Tommy Two Moons came galloping into the semicircle of light. Behind him ran two panting police constables. Not far behind them, seated on an old and windbroken pony, was a fat sergeant, puffing with exertion.

Bill stood up and went to meet them.

'Riding Bill's horse was great,' said Tommy Two Moons, flinging himself into the chair alongside Sam. 'You should have seen me fly.'

'Glad you had fun,' said Sam, listening to the low rumble of voices behind them.

'Oh, I had fun all right. I reckon I woke up every house in town with the clattering of hooves on the road.'

Tommy's words were cut short by the arrival of Buffalo Bill, followed by the three policemen. They moved across to the bound and gagged body of Morgan Stanfield. The two constables hauled him to his feet and took off the gag.

'Thank God you've come,' panted Stanfield. 'They tried to kill me, all of them. They just dived on me, a dozen of them, beat me to a pulp.'

Sam stared open-mouthed.

Buffalo Bill shook his head at the captive. 'It won't work, Morgan. I've told them all about it. You're going to the police station.'

'Thank heavens for that,' said Stanfield. 'I'll go anywhere if I can be safe from all of you.'

The police sergeant pointed towards the prisoner's ankles. 'Can you untie his feet, sir?'

Bill looked doubtful. 'Are you sure?' he asked. 'The man's dangerous – it took a dozen of my lads to knock him down and hold him.'

'Well, sir,' said the sergeant. 'I'm not going to carry him to the station. And neither are my men. The inspector will want to interview him first thing tomorrow morning and the station is the best place for him tonight, I reckon. Unless you want to keep him here?'

Bill shook his head quickly. 'No thanks. You take him.'

'Good,' said the sergeant. 'So untie his feet.'

'But he'll run!' gasped Sam. 'You can't let him go!'

'Sam's right!' exclaimed Running Water.

'He's in police custody now, and we'll take care of him,' grunted the sergeant, staring around the camp while the rough-riders worked on Stanfield's ropes. 'So this is the famous Wild West show. Maybe I'll have to come out and see your performance tomorrow.'

'I'll bring along some tickets for you and the men,' said Bill. 'All free, of course. With my compliments.'

The sergeant nodded, gravely. 'Fine. Thank you, sir. Ready, lads? Off to the station it is. He'll spend a night in the cells, then we'll see what tomorrow brings.'

Annie was on her feet in an instant. 'What do you mean, see what tomorrow brings? You don't intend to let him go?'

The sergeant stared at her, unmoved. 'I mean we'll see what tomorrow brings. That's what I said and that's what I meant.' He straightened himself up self-importantly. 'I don't judge these things. I just do my duty and leave the decisions to my superiors.'

The show people watched as Morgan Stanfield was led away, walking easily between the two constables. The sergeant followed them on his long-suffering pony.

Bill glanced quickly at Annie, then at Sam. 'Don't worry. They'll never let him go. I'll be at the police station first thing in the morning. I'll talk to this inspector. I'll make him see sense.' He paused and Sam could see the uncertainty in his eyes.

'Don't worry, Sam,' said Annie, reaching over to squeeze his knee. 'The sergeant didn't mean anything. That's just the way policemen talk. Nobody in their right mind would let a lowlife like Morgan Stanfield go free – not with all the evidence we've got against him. It really is all over.'

Sam stared at the fast-disappearing back of the murderer. He shuddered as he noticed that Stanfield wasn't even handcuffed, simply walking freely between the two policemen. What was wrong with the people in this place? Were they really that overconfident? Did they really think they knew best in everything?

Even as he watched, Morgan Stanfield turned his head and cast a malevolent glance back at the group outside Buffalo Bill's wagon. Hatred and fury blazed through the night and Sam knew, in that instant, that it was very far from over.

Chapter Eight

THE DEADWOOD STAGE

Buffalo Bill was as good as his word. He was away early the next morning, heading for the town police station with tickets for the show. Sam had slept little and was up and about as soon as day broke. He was carrying a large bucket of water from the stream when he saw Bill climb down from his wagon. The showman was dressed in his best buckskin jacket, his hair neatly combed and curled. 'We'll get this sorted out,' he said, 'and then we can get on doing what we do best – running a Wild West show.'

Sam watched him stride away. The man was clearly a lot more confident than he was. Perhaps the American police were better than the ones in Sam's experience. He waited until Bill had left the showground, then he turned and walked slowly towards Star's tepee.

'Breakfast,' announced Star, clapping him on the shoulder and guiding him towards a chair alongside the fire. 'Got to keep your strength up, eh?'

Sam and Running Water sat silently, picking at the food that Star had prepared. Neither of them spoke or had much appetite for the meal. Sam knew that, like him, the girl was thinking about the events of the previous night.

'I don't know,' said Star, gathering up the remnants of the food and tossing them to the dogs that always hung around the Indian village waiting for scraps. 'I slave over a hot fire and nobody eats a thing.'

'Sorry,' said Sam.

Star smiled at him, and then glanced up at the sky. 'I reckon the weather's looking pretty bad,' she said. 'I just hope it holds off for the show this afternoon.'

She was right. At that moment a warm breeze was blowing but there were large deep clouds, grey and menacing, gathering in the west, far out over the sea. Sam was no weather expert but he guessed there would be rain later in the day.

'There's Bill,' said Running Water, suddenly. 'He didn't take very long at the police station.'

Buffalo Bill was standing by the entrance to the showground. Sam and Running Water got to their feet and joined him just as Annie Oakley came out of her wagon.

'Goddam useless,' Bill stormed. 'What's the matter with the police in this country?'

Annie took him by the arm and led him to the long wooden bench that stood alongside her wagon. 'Tell me,' she said.

Bill stared at her. 'He's gone,' he said, shortly. 'Stanfield's gone.'

'You mean they let him go? They released him?'

Bill nodded his head. He glanced quickly at Sam and Running Water. ''Fraid so. Don't know how he did it but he convinced the inspector it was all part of a feud between him and us showfolk, said we were trying to make trouble for him. Anyway, he's gone and God knows where he's hiding out.'

'But why didn't they wait for you?' asked Annie.

Bill shrugged. 'Your guess is as good as mine.'

Sam felt the horror in his belly and throat. The day, already grey and dark, seemed more oppressive than ever.

'I'll get some of the boys to search the town for him,' said Buffalo Bill. 'But if I know Morgan they won't find hide nor hair of him. He's far too clever for that.' He paused and glanced at Sam. 'You're at risk, kid. My guess is, sooner or later, he'll come looking for you. Now that he knows where you are.' He stood up and placed his hand on Sam's shoulder. 'He'll come looking for revenge, that's my guess. You all heard what he thinks about my family. He wants revenge on all of us, but Sam's his biggest threat.'

He thought for a moment, considering what to do. At last he came to a decision. 'Now listen, all of you. We're here today and for most of tomorrow. Sam, you'd better lie low for a while, stay out of the way until we break the show tomorrow afternoon. I'll put a couple of the boys to guard your wagon – he won't get past them. Don't worry, son. It will all work out.'

Later that day Bill sent the two biggest and strongest rough-riders to stand guard over Star's wagon – and over Sam. 'Just keep the coffees coming,' joked one of them. 'Then forget we're here.' He flexed his muscles and Sam tried hard to grin back at him.

That afternoon the show went on as planned, Tommy Two Moons tossing the glass balls into the air for Bill. There was no sign of Morgan Stanfield. When Sam awoke late at night, fear clutching at his throat, he saw the giant shadow of one of the rough-riders sitting easily outside the wagon, and felt better.

Late the next day, they left Pembroke Dock. The long line of wagons headed northwards in a snaking column, their harnesses jangling and the pack of dogs yelping and racing alongside. Aberystwyth was their next destination and Bill had allowed two days for the journey.

The bad weather that Star had predicted for the previous day had not arrived, strong winds from the north-east keeping the rain clouds hovering offshore. But as they turned the horses' heads to the north, great globules of rain began to fall. Within minutes the rain was streaming down, bouncing off the ground with a ferocity that amazed everyone.

'I thought it could rain on the Great Plains,' said Summer Storm. 'This is worse, a lot worse.'

'This is Wales,' said Sam. 'And believe me, the rain gets a lot heavier than this. You've got the right names: Summer Storm, Running Water.'

Star shuddered as a squall of rain lashed at her face. She promptly gave up her seat next to the driver and retired to the back of the wagon. There she sat, singing some interminable Cherokee song to Tommy and Summer.

'I'm going outside,' said Sam. 'Between Star's singing and the rain on the canvas I can't hear myself think.' He pulled a piece of sacking over his shoulders and arranged another around his legs. Then he climbed out of the front of the wagon. The driver, already soaked and with rain dripping off the end of his nose, was happy to see him. 'Let me have a piece of that sacking, son?' he drawled.

Sam passed across one of the sacks. Soon Running Water joined them, carrying more pieces of sacking. They were heavy and kept most of the rain off their clothes.

They sat comfortably on the wagon in the gloom as the caravan jolted on its way. The smell of the rain on the parched earth was musty, mingling with the sweet tang of the pine chips that had once been carried in the sacks.

Sam was glad to be away from Pembroke Dock and the threat of Morgan Stanfield. He supposed the man could come after him, following the show up the length of Wales but tried to convince himself that it wasn't likely. 'You don't think he'll come after me, do you?' he said to Running Water. 'If I was Stanfield I'd get on the boat to Ireland and keep out of the way.'

'I don't know,' she commented. 'You heard what Bill said about him. And you are still the only witness to that murder. Maybe the police will change their minds and try to arrest him.'

'I don't think so,' said Sam. 'You saw what they were like the other night. No, he's free and he's going to stay free.'

Their journey took them over the wild and rugged Preseli mountains, huge outcrops of rock that gleamed black as coal under the constant rain. The wind howled in off the sea, pulling wildly at the canvas coverings of the wagons. The snap of the taut, soaked canvas made Sam jump each time it flapped and cracked.

'Sure is one hell of a wild country you've got here,' laughed the wagon driver as they finally started the drop down towards Fishguard. 'Reminds me of the Rockies, the Rocky Mountains.'

Sam wasn't sure whether he was teasing. 'I'd like to see the Rockies,' he said.

They camped that night just south of Cardigan town, pulling the wagons into a circle alongside the river and not even bothering to put up the tents and tepees. There was no show to prepare and the people of the town kept sensibly indoors in such dreadful weather. Dinner was just cheese, cold meat and bread, washed down with a mug of water.

Sam awoke next morning to the sound of more singing from Star, this time from outside the wagon. The rain had gone and the day promised to be fine.

'Up and out, sleepyheads,' she called. 'It's a new day and there's work to be done.'

Their journey that morning could not have been more different. The sun shone and the breeze from the west was fresh and cooling. Even Star moved up to join them at the front of the wagon.

They travelled, most of that day, along cliff-top roads with wonderful views of the sea on their left. Far away in the distance, Sam could make out the shapes of tiny fishing boats and drifters running their nets along the seabed. The waves shone and sparkled in the clear air. In spite of Morgan Stanfield, in spite of all he had endured, it felt good to be alive.

The wind was light and fresh and they waved happily to the people in the towns and villages they passed. As evening began to draw in, they arrived at the showground in Aberystwyth.

'How do you say that name?' asked Running Water. 'Aber . . .'

Sam shook his head. He could just about manage names like Cardiff and Swansea; Aberystwyth was way beyond him.

As always, a crowd of spectators quickly gathered to watch them setting up camp. Afterwards, many of them stayed on to wander past the tepees and the campfires that glowed yellow and red in the dusk. It was something Sam had become used to over the months he had been with the show but today he hung back, seeking the safety of the tepee.

'What's wrong?' asked Running Water, her eyes questioning.

'There's just so many people about,' said Sam. 'Stanfield could be out there, amongst them all. We'd never spot him in a crowd like that.'

Running Water laid her hand on his arm. 'Stop worrying, Sam. I don't think Morgan Stanfield will have followed us here. We've left him well behind.'

Perhaps, thought Sam. When he was thinking about it sensibly, without panic, he could see that the killer would have to be mad to chase him here. There would simply be no point. But then the fear would bubble up again. He couldn't get rid of it. It plagued him like toothache and, just like a bad tooth, he kept going back to probe the problem time and time again.

Finally, around eleven, Star announced it was time for bed. The wagon had been divided into several sleeping compartments by long pieces of wood that broke up the space into a series of tiny bedrooms which gave each of them a degree of privacy.

'Try to get some sleep,' Running Water advised.

Sam nodded, not particularly hopefully. But to his surprise, as soon as his head came down onto his bedroll he fell instantly asleep and did not dream.

The following day was taken up with preparing for the show and Sam had no time to worry about Morgan Stanfield.

'Reckon you can throw the balls today?' Bill asked as he and Sam tramped back to the wagons for lunch.

Sam nodded eagerly – anything to get back to normality.

The show went well and no matter how hard he tried, no matter how sneakily he tossed up the targets, he could not fool Bill. The veteran showman seemed to be able to shoot the glass balls no matter how or when they were thrown. Sam had never been completely sure about Running Water's story about Bill's foolproof guns but he'd never once been able to trick him.

'Good try,' Bill laughed when they had finished in the show ring. 'Keep it up – one day you might catch me out.'

Sam grinned at him and a warm glow of contentment filled his belly. For the first time in his life, he felt accepted as part of one big family. That night he relaxed for the first time in days as he sat with Running Water outside the wagon, breathing in the mild scents of the autumn night.

'You all right?' asked the girl.

Sam smiled and nodded. 'If he was coming, he'd have come last night, don't you think?'

Running Water said nothing. They sat on, watching the stars, hoping to see a comet blaze across the cloudless sky. Buffalo Bill had told them there was a good chance of seeing shooting stars here in the west. They watched until their necks ached, but nothing appeared.

Finally Running Water stood up and turned towards the wagon. 'I'm off to bed,' she said.

'I'm not sleepy,' said Sam. 'I think I'll stay up a while. You never know, I might get lucky and get to see one of those shooting stars.'

Running Water yawned goodnight and climbed, heavily, into the wagon.

Sam fixed his gaze on the heavens, determined to be the first to tell Buffalo Bill he'd sighted a comet. But the day had been a long one and, before long, his eyes were shutting and his head was nodding.

When he awoke it was dark, with a thin sliver of crescent moon and a sprinkling of stars in the night sky. At first Sam wasn't sure where he was, but soon realised, from the stiffness in his limbs, that he must have been asleep for a few hours.

How quiet it was, how peaceful. In the darkness he could just make out the shapes of the sleeping wagons. His people, he thought gratefully, lulled by the distant sound of waves breaking against the shingle.

He was very nearly asleep again when a sharper sound broke across the stillness. Crack! It could have been a twig snapping or, Sam realised with a start, the sound of breaking glass. It came from the direction of the Deadwood Stage, he was almost sure. Suddenly he was wide awake.

Just why he went to investigate without summoning help, Sam never knew, but that's what he did. He stole between the wagons and the tepees, brushing against their canvas awnings, until he reached Buffalo Bill's wagon, bigger and more ornate than the others. In the darkness, Sam half stumbled but steadied himself against the carved edge of one of the shafts. He didn't really want to rouse Bill unless he had to and guessed that the showman was probably sleeping heavily after enjoying a glass or two of whisky before settling down for the night.

Sam moved softly around the back of the wagon, where he could just make out the dark outline of the Deadwood Stage. He moved closer.

'Stop right there,' came a sudden harsh whisper from behind him. 'Don't make a sound. Not if you value your life.' The voice was low but light in tone and Sam felt the sharp prick of a knife at his back as a man's arm locked itself around his neck.

'Move,' said the voice. 'Quickly, quietly.'

Man and boy moved jerkily through the empty, silent showground, past the dark shadowy wagons and the tepees reaching up like giant fingers into the night sky. Sam shivered but he knew it was not from the cold.

'Walk. But make sure you do it nice and slow.'

Sam moved off, the knife blade cutting into his back. The sorrow was huge in his chest. He was lost and he knew it.

Chapter Nine

SHOWDOWN

As he pushed and pulled Sam along the silent streets of Aberystwyth, Morgan Stanfield did not open his mouth to say anything but the sharp stabbing of his knife in the small of Sam's back spoke far more eloquently than any words.

The streets were empty and echoing, the only sound coming from the ringing of Stanfield's boots on the cobbles, the man's laboured breathing and the low grating roar of waves on the seashore. They saw no one, only their own dancing shadows on the pavement and walls.

At last they approached the bridge across the Rheidol river. Stanfield pulled to a halt and dragged Sam off the road, down onto the riverbank. 'I reckon we need a break,' he said, blowing heavily. 'I must be more out of condition than I thought. No problem, none of your friends in the show will be awake just yet. No need to rush things.'

Sam stared at the man as he recovered his breath. 'Why are you doing this?' he demanded. 'How did you get here?'

Stanfield shrugged his broad shoulders. 'Does it matter? I was behind you all the way up the coast, you and that infernal wagon train. You were so easy to follow. All I had to do was keep well back, so I wasn't spotted. But I had you in my sights the whole way up from Pembroke Dock.'

'But why? What can you get out of kidnapping me?'

Stanfield stretched out one hand, reached deep into his pocket and brandished a wad of banknotes. 'Don't kid yourself that I was after you, boy. I'm on my way to Liverpool and a boat back to the good old USA, but first I needed to reclaim some of my personal property.' He paused and jerked the knife towards Sam's throat.

The boy pulled back in alarm. 'You mean you came to rob Buffalo Bill.'

'Robbery? That's hardly what I'd call it, just claiming back something for my family, some of the money Bill Cody's poppa and his people cheated from us. And nobody would have known I'd been there until you came snooping about.'

'Let me go. I won't tell.'

Morgan Stanfield laughed. 'You have got to be kidding me. No, you're a complication I didn't bank on. I haven't decided what to do about you just yet though. But whether I kill you sooner or later, we'll have to see. You might turn out to be useful to me, a bit of insurance. And besides, there's the small question of revenge.'

Sam knew it wasn't just idle talk. If he thought Sam was useful, Stanfield might keep him alive, at least for a little while. But he didn't deceive himself. When his usefulness was over Stanfield would kill him.

'Revenge,' said Stanfield smoothly, 'is such a satisfying emotion, don't you think? I owe you, boy, so don't think there's any quick or easy way out of this.'

After about five minutes he jerked Sam roughly to his feet. 'Keep it slow, boy,' he snarled. 'We've got a long way to go.'

Sam trudged along bitterly. He tried not to think of Star and Running Water sleeping in the wagon, blissfully unaware of his danger. When they woke in an hour or so they would find him gone – and Bill Cody's money – and what hurt most was the idea that the show people would think badly of him. As far as they were concerned he'd be nothing more than a runaway thief. He could have cried with the pain of it.

Soon they were walking along the seafront, along the wide promenade with its elegant pier and, at the northern end, the knotted fist of Constitution Hill. Beyond lay the mountains of mid Wales.

They made slow and awkward progress, Stanfield holding Sam in a vice-like grip and stopping repeatedly to look back over his shoulder. 'Someone's following us,' he muttered at last. 'I can sense it. Somebody's on to us.' He stood and glared behind him, his hand still on Sam's shoulder and the knife hovering dangerously. Sam followed his gaze but he saw no one.

After a while Stanfield relaxed his grip. 'You'd better hope I'm imagining it, boy. For your sake.' They moved on along the promenade. When they were almost at the foot of Constitution Hill, Stanfield glanced back once more. And this time his head jerked up and he swore. 'Damn it! I was right. There must be seven or eight of them.'

Desperately he scanned his surroundings and his eyes fell on the rugged headland behind them. 'Up here,' he said. 'Come on.' He dragged Sam across the road and onto the grass and rocks of Constitution Hill. Slowly they began to climb, Stanfield pushing the boy before him. Soon they were fifty feet up and the climb was growing steadily steeper.

Sam's head was spinning. He had never liked heights and now, when he glanced down, the rocks and the sea beyond shimmered in the weak light of a new day. He staggered and almost fell, clutching at the grass to keep his balance.

'Steady, boy,' said Stanfield. 'For the first time I really do need to keep you alive – at least for a while.'

A sharp whistle echoed from the ground below and a voice cut through the darkness. 'Morgan, stop, give it up.'

Sam recognised the voice of Buffalo Bill. He could hardly believe it. There was hope after all.

Morgan Stanfield glared down at the people

below. 'Bill Cody. I knew it would be you. You just go to hell, Bill; this is one sharpshooting contest you're not going to win. You come any closer and I'll throw the boy off the cliff.'

He grabbed hold of Sam and pushed him out over the cliff edge. Sam's feet scrabbled for a hold but he knew that it was only Stanfield's grip that kept him from falling, from plummeting like a rock to the ground below.

'Get back, Bill,' Stanfield called, 'all of you. Let me see you heading down the road. You've got one minute, then the boy takes a dive.' He paused and Sam heard his mocking words echo clearly through the morning air. 'Go, Bill, go quickly. You don't want the boy's death on your conscience, do you?'

Fifty feet below, Sam could see Buffalo Bill and the others, their heads close together in urgent conference. They seemed to be arguing. But at last Bill stepped forward and held up his hands. 'All right, Morgan, you win. We're going. Just don't hurt the boy.'

Morgan Stanfield grinned and pulled Sam back, holding him now in front of his body – a shield from anyone gazing up from below. Sam ached with disappointment but he knew that Bill couldn't have said or done anything else.

'Bye bye, Billy Boy,' Stanfield called. 'Remind me to send you a postcard when I get back to the States.' Then he pulled Sam close and whispered in his ear. 'And there goes your last hope, boy.'

Bill and the rest of the group turned reluctantly around and began to move away down the promenade. Morgan Stanfield let out a great sigh of relief and pushed Sam to one side. At that second one of the group below spun round and pointed up at Stanfield. Dimly, Sam realised that it was Annie Oakley and she wasn't just pointing, she was aiming a rifle.

A crack split the early-morning air. Morgan Stanfield gasped and jerked back against the cliff face. His hands scrabbled at his leg and Sam saw a huge crimson stain beginning to spread across his thigh. 'No,' he gasped. 'No.'

Then he staggered and began to pitch forward and fall. Instinctively, Sam reached out and grabbed at the man's coat. Stanfield swung around, smashing into the cliff face. The pain in Sam's arm was intense but, by some miracle, he managed to hang on.

'Help me, boy,' Stanfield gasped. 'Don't let me go.'

Sam gritted his teeth. He had no intention of letting go – Morgan Stanfield had a date with judge and jury and Sam wanted to make sure he kept it.

'Stay still, Sam,' called Bill Cody from below. 'Don't move. We're coming to get you.'

Moving was the last thing on Sam's mind. He held tightly to a clump of grass with one hand, the other twisted into the fabric of Morgan Stanfield's coat. At last, two of the rough-riders managed to climb the hill and slowly, carefully, gain a hold on Stanfield's body. They tied a rope around his chest and lowered him down to the men waiting below. Then they helped Sam down.

At the foot of the hill, Running Water was waiting with Annie Oakley and Bill. Sam smiled weakly at her.

'I woke and wondered where you were. When I couldn't find you, I raised the alarm. Then Bill found that money was missing . . . he sent out search parties in all directions . . . but you were so far ahead of us . . .'

They stared at Morgan Stanfield, now tied hand and foot and covered with a coat from one of the rough-riders. The killer did not look at them or speak. Sam felt his legs go suddenly weak. He felt sick, his head swam and he staggered to one side.

'Sit down, Sam,' said Buffalo Bill. 'It's just shock. It'll go in a while.' They squatted on the grass while someone ran for the police.

Running Water reached out and squeezed Sam's hand. 'It really is the end this time,' she said. 'You're safe at last.'

Sam nodded, relief coursing through his body.

Then he felt Annie Oakley nudging him with her shoulder. 'I'll tell you what, Sam, that was one hell of a shot I made.' She turned to Bill Cody. 'What do you reckon, Bill? Good, wasn't it?'

Bill shook his head and grinned at her. 'Not bad, Annie, not bad at all.'

Annie was not going to let the great Buffalo Bill off

the hook quite so easily. This was her moment and she was going to enjoy it. 'Not bad? That was a shot in a million – in the half light, at that distance. I tell you, this proves one thing. I really am a better shot than you.'

Bill bristled and for a moment he and Annie glared at each other. Then a small, slow smile spread across his face and he shrugged. 'Maybe,' he said. 'Maybe it does.'

Chapter Ten

DECISION TIME

The Wild West show was detained in Aberystwyth for several days while the police conducted their investigation and trawled through every tiny detail of the shooting. They weren't at all happy about people taking the law into their own hands, and for a while it even looked as if Annie might be taken into custody and charged with attempted murder.

She and Bill Cody and Sam spent long hours at the police station, trying to put their side of the case to officers who, at first, were very unwilling to accept their story. Happily Stanfield's injury turned out to be a flesh wound only and, when the police searched him and found the stolen money, it helped to confirm Buffalo Bill's story. The police agreed to investigate the murder accusation by writing to their colleagues in Cardiff.

Sam and the others were sent back to the Indian village and the wagon train with strict instructions that they were not to leave town.

Sam was interviewed three separate times by the Aberystwyth police. He was terrified that his Cardiff past would catch up with him but it was clear that the real interest was centred on Bill and Annie. On the afternoon of the last day they were brought once more to the office of the investigating officer.

'A bunch of cowboys!' complained the police inspector. 'Just where do you think you are? The Wild West? Just what the devil did you think you were doing?'

'Saving someone's life,' said Bill, his eyes twinkling.

Bill's good humour and easy nature cut no ice with the inspector. 'This was a police matter. You should have left it to us,' he insisted.

Bill thought it wiser not to say what had happened the last time they'd left matters to the Welsh constabulary, in Pembroke Dock.

It took a while for the Cardiff force to confirm the details of Mr Tomkins's death, but at last there was enough evidence for Stanfield to be charged with both theft and murder.

Annie was finally free to go. And so was Buffalo Bill Cody.

The police inspector escorted them out of the station and pointed his finger down the road. 'Get out of here,' he said. 'Get back to your Wild West show. But remember, if any of you – and I mean anyone – so much as breathes out of turn again, I'll lock you up and throw away the key.'

*

Back at the showground Sam and Running Water were waiting outside Bill's wagon.

Buffalo Bill waved them to follow him inside, where they settled themselves on a brightly coloured Indian blanket. 'It's all over,' Bill said, explaining that this time Stanfield would remain in police custody. 'We're free to go, soon as we're ready. And do you know something? I'll be really glad to leave this place. It's got too many bad memories.'

'I agree,' said Sam, getting up, ready to go at once.

'There is one thing,' said Annie, suddenly.

Everyone stared at her.

'What are we going to do about this young man? He comes from Cardiff, not America. When we go back to the States in a few weeks' time, what's going to become of him? We can't just let him loose on the streets again, can we?'

'No, ma'am,' said Star, coming up the steps of the wagon behind her. 'It's Sam's choice but, if he wants it, there's always room for him in my wagon. He's become part of the family.'

Sam stared at her. He had never thought about what might happen once Morgan Stanfield was out of the way. He had lived from day to day for so long now that he had never even thought about the future. 'Thank you, Star,' he said.

'There's always room for him in the Wild West show, too,' said Bill. 'After all, nobody throws those balls quite like Sam. Look, son, I guess we need to put our cards on the table. We'd all like you to stay with us. As Star said, you've become one of the family. But we can't force you. It's got to be your decision. Think about it – you don't have ties in this country, no family, do you?'

Sam shook his head. 'No, sir, there's nobody.'

'All righty,' said Bill. 'Why not come with us to a new country, make a fresh start. It seems simple enough to me but, like I say, it's a choice only you can make. You wouldn't be the first Welshman to start a new life out in America!'

Sam stared at Running Water. She was sitting with her head bowed, not looking at him, and for a few moments Sam thought she might be angry with Star and Bill.

And then she looked up and he saw the tears in her eyes. 'Please stay,' she whispered. 'You're the best friend I've ever had. Stay with the show, Sam. Come with us back to America.'

Sam tried to smile but, instead, the sudden catch in his throat brought him to the edge of tears. He had never known such kindness or such friendship, and it humbled him. He nodded and, at last, managed to find his voice. 'Yes, please, I'd love to stay. I'd love to see America. And one day, Bill, I'm going to be shooting those glass balls out of the air instead of you.'

Everyone laughed and Sam Speed (formerly Thomas) knew that, at last, he had found his home and family.

For the Historical Record

Buffalo Bill brought his Wild West show to Britain three times – in 1887, in 1891 and in 1903 – 1904 (the period covered by this story). He did not come to Wales on his first visit, which was to help celebrate Queen Victoria's Golden Jubilee. On his second visit he enjoyed a huge success in Cardiff and this prompted him to return, this time for a full tour of Wales in 1903 and 1904.

It is hard to know how to describe the effect he and the show had on the people of Britain. Put simply, they had never seen anything like it.

In the days before television, before computer graphics, before blue-screen technology and the cinema, the Wild West show was the most exciting thing they had ever experienced. It was a cross between a circus, the best laser show ever invented and a trip on a rocket ship to the moon.

People flocked to the show in their thousands and came away with visions of cowboys and the Wild West that would stay with them for the rest of their lives. Nobody who saw the show ever forgot the colours, the sights, the sheer spectacle of it all – which, of course, was exactly what Buffalo Bill wanted. Hopefully, I have managed to catch at least some of that splendour in this story.

In describing the original inhabitants of America – men, women and children who made up a large part of the Wild West show – I found I had a problem. To Buffalo Bill and his companions, to the ordinary members of the public in the nineteenth and early twentieth centuries, they were Indians – Red Indians. Nowadays we are quite clear: the correct term is Native Americans.

It wouldn't be politically correct to use the terms 'Indian' or 'Red Indian' these days but they are right for the time when the story took place. I apologise for this but hope that readers will understand that the phrase Native American is the correct one.

I have also changed, slightly, some of the dates and times – and the order – that the show visited certain towns. This is, as film makers say, for dramatic purposes. I make no apologies for these changes as this is a story which interweaves fictional events and characters with the historical facts.

Although Buffalo Bill was a real character, he would have thoroughly approved of mixing fact and fiction as his own life was an amazing blend of adventure and theatre. Just to set the record straight, these are the facts we know about the real William Cody.

William was born in Iowa in 1846 but lived for several years in Canada. His mother and father, whose family came from Quaker roots and who were fiercely opposed to slavery, had moved to Canada from America where slavery was still legal. They moved back to America, to Kansas, when William was a child. At that time the people of Kansas were sharply divided over slavery and the Cody family was persecuted by pro-slavery supporters. This forced William's father to spend a lot of his time away from home. On one occasion William learned of a plot to kill him and rode thirty miles to warn him of the danger. His father's luck ran out when he gave an anti-slavery speech and was seriously wounded. He never really recovered from this injury and it contributed to his early death.

After his father died, young Bill Cody took a job as a 'boy extra' with a wagon train. This meant riding up and down the line of covered wagons, delivering messages to the drivers and workmen. As a young man, Cody worked as a scout for the US army and received a medal for his services. He got his nickname 'Buffalo Bill' when he had a contract to supply the Kansas Pacific Railroad with buffalo meat, killing over 4,000 buffalo in eighteen months. He served on the Union (Yankee) side in the American Civil War and as Chief of Scouts during the Plains Wars against the Native Americans.

In later life, Buffalo Bill claimed to have had many jobs, including being a trapper, a gold prospector, a Pony Express rider, wagonmaster, stagecoach driver and manager of a hotel.

These days, Buffalo Bill is probably most famous

for his Wild West show. He recruited performers from all over the world. His shows began with a horseback parade and visitors would see many different feats of equestrian skill. Real historical celebrities took part, including the Native American Indian chief Sitting Bull with twenty of his braves, and the legendary Annie Oakley. Even though he'd fought against them, Buffalo Bill learned to respect Native Americans in his days as a frontier scout, and he supported their rights. He employed many more natives than Sitting Bull, and believed that his show offered them good pay for a better life. He regarded them as his friends and fellow Americans, which was quite unusual at the time, and he blamed any violence which involved them on the promises and treaties broken by the government. Buffalo Bill was also ahead of his time in supporting women's rights as he believed that people should be paid the same rate for the same work.

His shows included re-enactments of the Pony Express, stagecoach robberies, and Indian attacks on wagon trains and settlers' cabins. He performed in front of Queen Victoria and King George V as well as the German Kaiser Wilhelm II. His shows were enormously successful in Europe and Bill became an international celebrity.

Back home, he founded the town of Cody in Wyoming, opening a hotel and establishing a ranch where he bred cattle. The herds of bison which had once roamed the plains were now threatened with extinction and Buffalo Bill became involved in conservation projects, and eventually a dam, the Buffalo Bill Dam, was renamed in his honour.

Buffalo Bill died in 1917.

About the Author

Phil Carradice is a freelance writer, consultant and broadcaster. He regularly holds creative writing workshops in schools and colleges. A former teacher and headteacher, he comes from Pembroke Dock, but now lives in the Vale of Glamorgan. Phil has a strong interest in history and writes a regular blog for the BBC Wales website.

www.bbc.co.uk/blogs/wales/authors/Phil_Carradice

More stories by Phil Carradice

Saving SS Shannon

When William hides from the school bully on the wreck of an old ship, he cannot imagine the adventures ahead of him . . . or the dangers! His tormentor's father is a property developer with big plans for the dockyard area – and they don't include the *SS Shannon*. Some say the old steamship is haunted. Is William brave enough to stand up to the bullies . . . and save the *SS Shannon* from certain destruction?

The Black Chair

Danny raised his arm to show the wound stripes on his sleeve. 'German machine gun at Passchendaele. Three bullets in the thigh and groin.'

With injuries serious enough to get him sent home to Wales – and his beloved Angharad – Danny's recovery cannot really begin until he has fulfilled a promise to a friend. For that he must travel north to the National Eisteddfod at Birkenhead, where the appearance of a black-draped Bardic Chair chills the audience . . .

This is Phil Carradice's tribute to Ellis Evans, better known by his bardic name, Hedd Wyn, and to all those young men who lost their lives in the First World War. A work of fiction, *The Black Chair* draws on careful research for its military authenticity and its determination to convey the suffering and courage of a lost generation.